THE
SIGNMAKER'S ASSISTANT

TEDD ARNOLD

THE SIGNMAKER's ASSISTANT

DIAL BOOKS FOR YOUNG READERS • NEW YORK

For Doug and his assistant Andrew

Published by Dial Books for Young Readers
A Division of Penguin Books USA Inc.
375 Hudson Street
New York, New York 10014

Printed in Hong Kong
by South China Printing Company (1988) Limited
Typography by Nancy R. Leo
First Edition
3 5 7 9 10 8 6 4 2

Library of Congress Cataloging in Publication Data
Arnold, Tedd.
The signmaker's assistant/by Tedd Arnold.
p.   cm.
Summary: A young signmaker's apprentice dreams of having his
own sign shop but creates havoc when he is left in charge by himself.
ISBN 0-8037-1010-0 (trade). — ISBN 0-8037-1011-9 (library)
[1. Signs and signboards—Fiction.]   I. Title.
PZ7.A7379S1 1992   [E]—dc20   90-19537   CIP   AC

The art for this book was created using watercolor paint
and colored pencil. It was then color-separated and reproduced
as red, blue, yellow, and black halftones.

Everyone in town agreed. The old signmaker did the finest work for miles around. Under his brush ordinary letters became beautiful words—words of wisdom, words of warning, or words that simply said which door to use.

When he painted STOP, people stopped because the sign looked so important. When he painted PLEASE KEEP OFF THE GRASS, they kept off because the sign was polite and sensible. When he painted GOOD FOOD, they just naturally became hungry.

People thanked the signmaker and paid him well. But the kind old man never failed to say, "I couldn't have done it without Norman's help."

Norman was the signmaker's assistant. Each day after school he cut wood, mixed colors, and painted simple signs.

"Soon I will have a shop of my own," said Norman.

"Perhaps," answered the signmaker, "but not before you clean these brushes."

One day, after his work was done, Norman stood at a window over the sign shop and watched people. They stopped at the STOP sign. They entered at the ENTER sign. They ate under the GOOD FOOD sign.

"They do whatever the signs say!" said Norman to himself. "I wonder..." He crept into the shop while the signmaker napped. With brush and board he painted a sign of his own.

Early the next morning he put up the sign, then ran back to his window to watch.

"No school?" muttered the principal. "How could I forget such a thing?"

"No one informed me," said the teacher.

"Hooray!" cheered the children, and everyone went home.

"This is great!" cried Norman. He looked around town for another idea. "Oh," he said at last, "there is something I have always wanted to do."

The following day Norman jumped from the top of the fountain in the park. As he swam, he thought to himself, I can do lots of things with signs. Ideas filled his head.

That afternoon when Norman went to work, the signmaker said, "I must drive to the next town and paint a large sign on a storefront. I'll return tomorrow evening, so please lock up the shop tonight."

As soon as the signmaker was gone, Norman started making signs. He painted for hours and hours and hours.

In the morning people discovered new signs all around town.

Norman watched it all and laughed until tears came to his eyes. But soon he saw people becoming angry.

"The signmaker is playing tricks," they shouted. "He has made fools of us!"

The teacher tore down the NO SCHOOL TODAY sign. Suddenly people were tearing down all the signs—not just the new ones but every sign the signmaker had ever painted.

Then the real trouble started. Without store signs, shoppers became confused. Without stop signs, drivers didn't know when to stop. Without street signs, firemen became lost.

In the evening when the signmaker returned from his work in the next town, he knew nothing of Norman's tricks. An angry crowd of people met him at the back door of his shop and chased him into the woods.

As Norman watched, he suddenly realized that without signs and without the signmaker, the town was in danger.

"It's all my fault!" cried Norman, but no one was listening.

Late that night the signmaker returned and saw a light on in his shop.
Norman was feverishly painting.

While the town slept and the signmaker watched, Norman put up stop signs,
shop signs, street signs, danger signs, and welcome signs; in and out signs, large
and small signs, new and beautiful signs. He returned all his presents and cleared
away the garbage at the grocery store. It was morning when he finished putting
up his last sign for the entire town to see.

Then Norman packed his things and locked up the shop. But as he turned to go, he discovered the signmaker and all the townspeople gathered at the door.

"I know you're angry with me for what I did," said Norman with downcast eyes, "so I'm leaving."

"Oh, we were angry all right!" answered the school principal. "But we were also fools for obeying such signs without thinking."

"You told us you are sorry," said the signmaker, "and you fixed your mistakes. So stay, and work hard. One day this shop may be yours."

"Perhaps," answered Norman, hugging the old man, "but not before I finish cleaning those brushes."